SUSAN AND THE GANGSTER

A WILKINSON'S DETECTIVE AGENCY SHORT STORY

ALEXANDRIA BLAELOCK

Also by Alexandria Blaelock

SHORT STORY COLLECTIONS
The Haunting of Hayward Hall
Lovelorn, Lovestruck and Love at First Sight
Common or Garden Variety Heroes
Case Files of the Wilkinson Detective Agency
Unavoidable Fates
Christmas Travesties
Five Faces of Felicia Clarke

FICTION
That Love Nonsense
Taipan vs Brown

MS BLAELOCK'S BOOKS
Stress Free Dinner Parties
Signature Wardrobe Planning
Holistic Personal Finance
Minimally Viable Housekeeping
Planning a Life Worth Living

A SELECTION OF AVAILABLE SHORT STORIES
Alma'that thas Grace
Fate in Your Hands
Kiss of Death
Lady of the Looking Glass
Life in the Security Directorate
Morning Star, Evening Star, Superstar
Payton's Run
Secret Singer
Shining Star
Ship in a Bottle
Simone Says Hands in the Air
The Day the Schedule Broke

SUSAN AND THE GANGSTER

A WILKSINSON'S DETECTIVE AGENCY SHORT STORY

ALEXANDRIA BLAELOCK

BlueMere Books

MELBOURNE, AUSTRALIA

For permission requests, please contact
enquiries@bluemerebooks.com.

Ordering Information:
Discounts are available on quantity purchases. For details, contact orders@bluemerebooks.com.

Susan and the Gangster/Alexandria Blaelock
paperback ISBN: 978-1-922744-67-8
digital ISBN: 978-1-922744-68-5

Book Layout © BookDesignTemplates.com
Cover Art © Markus Schieder/Depositphotos

SUSAN AND THE GANGSTER

Susan stifled a yawn into her shoulder and rolled her eyes at Ryan, the colleague she was usually paired up with.

The briefing meeting was the boring as bat shit calm before the storm.

Mimma, their boss, had collected together the four teams who'd be primarily responsible for surveillance of Nick Liang.

She's been talking for an hour already, with the accompanying slide presentation detailing the information the background team had collected, and what the executive committee hoped they could achieve with additional surveillance.

"Our client has alleged Liang is the head of the criminal organisation who killed her son himself. Your job is to document every place he goes and every person he sees."

"Isn't that a job for the Police?" Ryan asked.

"Our client has not received satisfaction from the Police, and has engaged us to collect the necessary evidence.

"Any further questions?

"Then you have the weekend to yourselves and will commence this operation at 00:00 midnight Monday morning. It will run for one week, ending at 23:59 Sunday night.

"You are dismissed," she said and exited the meeting.

Susan stretched as she allowed the other attendees to leave the room. Why she'd ever thought working for the Wilkinson National Detective Agency (est. 1889), would be glamorous was beyond her.

The Collins Street offices were pretty nice, but she was rarely in them. More often than not she was outdoors, watching, trying not to be seen by others.

At least it was Summer, and it would be warm outside.

《《 • 》》

Susan stretched, closed her eyes, and turned to the sun hoping for a little extra oomph to recharge.

Not that there was much in the way of direct sun in the Bourke Street mall during the afternoon, but the rays reflecting from the shop windows would have to do.

According to her watch, there was a little over an hour until she clocked off, and if she was honest, she was exhausted.

Could not wait to hand over, and go home to a hot, spring blossom scented bath in her tiny bath, a glass of wine, and a Chinese take-out.

Quite possibly all at the same time while she listened to some smooth jazz, Norah Jones perhaps.

Not that her job was difficult *per se*, but following someone around, trying not to be conspicuous *was* quite tiring.

Which was why she always went nondescript for work; beige sundress, natural sandals, tortoiseshell sunglasses (not too big or small), no make-up, mouse-brown hair loosely tied in a ponytail at the back of her neck.

Absolutely nothing that might distinguish her during a casual scan of the crowd.

Except, for the keenly observant, she was almost always drawing in a sketch pad; her preferred way to keep track of the locations those she was tailing visited, and the people they met there.

Part life drawing, part Method of Loci memory palace for remembering details of interactions.

When pressed, as she had been once or twice, she would contend the mark was the most "unconventionally" attractive person she'd seen, and that was why she'd been following them.

Generally, the mark would call her a freak or a stalker, and tell her to leave; not necessarily quietly or politely.

Which she did, because the Agency always had teams of at least two people tailing the subjects of its investigations for just that reason.

It was a strategy that always worked, except *that* day.

She dropped her arms, and rolled her head backwards and forwards on her neck to ease the tension, and as she did, someone snatched the sketchbook from her lap.

She stood up, her eyes flicking open, ready to attack (in the nicest, most nondescript way) the person who'd taken the book.

Except.

It was the guy hanging out with the target.

She'd been made!

For a moment she was frozen, and it was just enough time for him to dance away, over the tram tracks with the book, flicking rapidly through the pages.

"I think she likes you," he called out to Nick, who looked amused because of course, everyone liked him.

And why wouldn't you when he wore a tight black t-shirt with black jeans and short black boots? When his shoulder-length dark hair shone with good health, and probably a lot of product too.

To go with the occasional glimpses of the silver stud in his ear and the heavy Bali silver chain he wore around his neck.

Following him around had been like watching an Asian drama live and in person. Everywhere he went, from café to market to supermarket people stopped to talk to him, and sometimes asked to have their photo taken with him.

If she didn't know better, she'd think he was an actor or something, knee-deep in admirers.

And that stupid guy was always with him. Though she'd only drawn one picture of him because he wasn't the target, and in about a millisecond that was going to get *really* embarrassing.

How the hell was she going to get out of this?

She couldn't leave the book with them; she hadn't remembered where he'd been, or who he'd been with. She hadn't needed to; it was all sketched out and she didn't need to remember it.

Not that the book identified her as a licensed private investigator, though she was required to carry her license when she was on the job.

But it did have her name, mobile phone number, and the post office box address of the Agency.

"Hey, these are pretty good," the guy said, showing them to Nick.

Oh my god, it just got worse and worse. This was going to be her off the case.

"Well, Susan Murray," said Nick, "can I buy you a drink?" as he started walking towards her.

Goddammit, she thought.

"Oh! No. I wouldn't dream of..."

Gak, try again, "I'm really not..."

Fuck's sake. "Just give me the book and I'll be on my way."

She took a step back as he and his cologne reached her, enveloping her in the smell of rainforest.

His hair fell down over his right eye as he smiled down at her, his warm brown eye meeting hers, looking every inch the cunning fist-fighting villain, the client suspected he was.

He smoothed a lock of hair that had escaped from her ponytail back, tucking it behind her ear.

Move, she thought-shouted at herself, don't stand here like a rabbit stuck in the oncoming car headlights!

He held his hand out behind him, and the other guy dropped the sketchbook in it, "you can only have it back if you let me buy you a drink."

She looked up at Nick, unable to break his gaze, weighing up the loss of a day's work with forcing her feet to turn around and walk away.

Stupid, stupid, stupid, she told herself.

He waggled the book, and she looked at it, and through it to Ryan on the other side of the mall.

She made a seemingly random coded gesture to tell him her cover was blown, and he nodded.

She looked back up at Nick and said, with bad grace "fine."

He smiled triumphantly, and grabbing her wrist, hustled her into a tiny restaurant tucked behind what used to be the main post office on the corner and was now a shopping arcade.

He ushered her into a booth and sat beside her, way too close.

Just when she thought she was on her own with him, and could maybe manage him, his friend sat opposite.

Not that he was any comfort, having got her into this mess he was unlikely to do anything to get her out of it.

In fact, it seemed to her that they had some kind of bet riding on whether he could get her to do… What?

Kiss him?

Sleep with him?

Take him back to her place?

Nick ordered wine and something to eat, not bothering to ask what she wanted.

He put the book on the table, and she made a grab for it.

"Ah ah ah-aa," he said, "not until you tell me why you were following us."

Good, she was prepared for that, "I just liked the way you moved," she shrugged, dipping her head as he quirked an eyebrow at his friend and slung his left arm along the back of the booth, and coincidentally around her.

Like a teenager at the movies.

She continued, "it's all kind of sharp and angled. Like a stick insect transformed into human form."

He smiled a small smile, as if she'd said something amusing, and then opened the book, carefully turning the pages, smoothing his fingers over himself on the page.

"I don't see anything sharp or angled about these drawings, I see the grace and form of a ballet dancer."

A curious way to describe himself.

"Ballet dancer? Really?" she attempted to pull the book across again, but he held it steady, resting his right forearm on it.

"You can't fool me," he said, "these pictures are not of an insect, but someone you're teetering on the edge of falling in love with."

Okay, that part was true.

She'd been following him around for a couple of days and hadn't seen anything that would suggest he was the kind of guy the client thought he was.

All she'd seen, was Nick being courteous and wildly charming.

His head leaned toward her, almost touching, and spoke quietly "did you think I wouldn't notice a woman as beautiful as you in a crowd?"

She lifted her head so rapidly it connected with his, his stubble grazing her temple.

Her cover had definitely been blown. Maybe as early as the first day.

And if he'd spotted her, he'd probably changed his pattern, and there wasn't anything she'd drawn that was compromising. Or in any way reliable.

Except perhaps his likeness.

And maybe his friend's.

It was time to extract herself and disappear before his suspicions were roused. If they weren't already.

And hopefully, the guys on the other shifts would get whatever evidence they needed.

Because as it turned out, she had nothing.

She stood up abruptly, "I have to go."

Nick leaned towards the table, blocking her path, "but we've only just got here."

"I forgot; I have somewhere I need to be."

"Not another man I hope? Though your sketchbook only captures me and Ares here," he nodded his head toward Ares, who grinned wolfishly.

And too late, she started to get worried she was in over her head. She held her handbag to her chest like a shield, looking around, trying to spot any other Wilkinson agents.

But she didn't see anyone she knew; from the Agency or otherwise.

Had they planned this? Had they stacked the restaurant?

Or even worse, had they infiltrated the Agency?

Was it possible she'd been placed there because someone thought she'd be relatively easy to crack?

Or disposable?

"No, I—"

As her sense of panic mounted, she realised she was hyperventilating and tried to slow her breathing.

"It's none of your business. You can keep the sketchbook."

She was prepared to climb over him if she had to, but at the last moment, he subsided, dropping his arm and pushing himself back towards the seat so she could scramble past.

And she fled, running out of the restaurant, not looking back and catching the nearest tram. Fortunately going in her direction.

After a few stops, she got off that tram, and onto the next one that arrived.

And a few stops after that, changed again.

Then walked for about twenty minutes to be sure no one was following her, but also to get to a tram stop where she could catch a tram that would take her home.

Sadly, her desire to relax in a hot bath had dissipated; she felt twitchy between her shoulder blades. Though she was fairly confident no one was following her.

But, she got off the tram a few stops earlier than usual and stopped in a busy restaurant. She managed to get a partially concealed table in a corner where she had a good view of the door.

She ordered a few dishes to make it look like she was waiting for someone, and a bottle of wine. She drank a glass and nibbled at the dishes, looking around as if she was expecting someone.

Which she kind of was, but had no idea how she would know them. Except that they'd probably take a seat facing the door like her.

About an hour and a half later she'd drunk all the wine, eaten a significant amount of food, and felt safe enough to walk the rest of the home without looking behind her.

That didn't stop her looking from the corner of her eyes at the streetscape reflected in the closed, darkened shops as she walked down the high street.

Gradually passing from shops and businesses to flats and houses, with less passing traffic.

Trying to move with her usual confident stride.

She hadn't expected to be out late, and hadn't brought a light cardigan, so she shivered a little in the cool evening air.

As she turned off the high street, she ran the last couple of blocks to her block of flats, dancing in the few seconds it took for her security code to register.

A quick glance back at the street, and she fled up the stairs, hoping no one would see which floor she lived on.

Back in her one and a half room flat, she crawled across the floor to avoid anyone seeing her from the street, and closed the curtains before she let herself relax a little.

Then she rang Wilkinson's and talked to the evening duty manager. She quickly outlined that her cover had been blown, and she was a little concerned Nick had the opportunity to discover who she was, where she worked, and where she lived.

"Don't worry," she was told, "we'll have someone drive by your flat a couple of times during the night. Stay home tomorrow morning and wait for your duty supervisor to call you. If anything happens in the meantime, call in again."

She smiled to herself as she acknowledged she was probably overreacting, but she still waited for several long minutes before lighting a couple of candles rather than switching on the main overhead lights.

And tried not to worry that he'd already been through her flat, or had one of those devices that could see through walls.

She crept over to the fridge and drank some milk from the plastic bottle before crawling to the bedroom to strip her clothes off and rest.

And as she fell asleep, she wondered if she'd been mistaken.

Was it possible, the client had some kind of grudge against Nick?

That he wasn't a thieving gangster? That he was just misunderstood.

And then told herself to get a grip on herself.

Nick Liang might be pretty, but his reputation was ruthless.

She was pretty sure she'd read somewhere that he beat a guy to death with his bare hands. Over a girl, or a parking spot, or something he imagined.

No matter what, she couldn't get involved in any capacity with him because she was a private investigator who was investigating him.

It was such a massive conflict of interest it would jeopardise the veracity of her evidence and testimony.

And ruin her career as an investigator.

And with the stain of Nick Liang around her, any career she chose to take up once he'd got bored and dumped her.

Though potentially, that would give her the opportunity to try making a living from her art.

Call herself Banksia and refuse to make public appearances.

She sighed and thumped her pillows to try and make them more comfortable. Eventually, she fell asleep but slept fitfully.

The next morning, she could see the sun shining through the gaps in the curtains, in what looked to be another beautiful day.

Which was almost a shame as she'd drunk too much the night before, and the day seemed rather brighter than normal.

She dragged on the luxurious black and gold silk robe her mother gave her last Christmas and padded to what passed as a kitchen in her bare feet to put her coffee percolator on.

Reflexively, she relaxed into her morning routine as she heard it start heating up. The smell of the fresh grounds from the jar was almost enough to keep her going until it was done.

She drank a big glass of water, cut up some sourdough and popped it in the toaster, got out some raw honey and cultured butter ready for when it popped.

On her way through to her tiny bathroom, she opened the curtains and windows.

And that was where the day started getting complicated because Nick Liang stood across the street, looking up.

She quickly took a step back away from the window, hoping he hadn't seen her, but afraid she couldn't be that lucky.

She rang her boss Mimma, and of course, the service diverted to the morning shift duty manager.

"Um, hi," she said. "It's Susan Murray from Day Surveillance Team five. I was assigned to watch Nick Liang last week, yesterday my cover was blown, and today he's right outside my house."

"I think I heard something about this in the briefing," she said, "please hold on," and before

Susan could say another word, she was listening to an electric organ version of some kind of cheerful, never-ending pop music that she hoped wasn't the same "tune" the clients heard.

Her toast popped, which was a teensy bit inconvenient as she still hadn't been to the bathroom.

She put her mobile phone on speaker on the kitchen bench, and danced a bit while she buttered the toast, and added honey, then poured herself a black coffee with one teaspoon of sugar; knocking the spoon once against the side of the jar to even it up before it went into the cup.

Not really game to leave the phone, and not sure how long until the woman came back, she took it, and her breakfast, across to her dining table to eat.

Not that it was a dining table, more of a large coffee table in front of the couch.

And when she'd finished, continued to sit while she licked her index finger and picked the crumbs up with it.

Finally, a man picked up the call, "Susan, it's Ben Hall here."

She sucked her breath in, because he was the partner she nominally worked for.

Her big, big... big boss.

"Ah, hello Ben."

"Your, er, situation... has given us what you might call a unique opportunity. If you're willing."

"An opportunity?"

"Yes. If Nick Liang is interested in you, it's possible you may gain deeper access to his network than we currently have access to. The kind of access where we can gather more information to prove or disprove the client's hypothesis and get this investigation wrapped up quicker than expected."

"But—"

"Now there could be some danger in this activity, and we're prepared to make you an acting Level Four operative for the duration. How does that sound?"

"It sounds like a promotion, but I haven't undertaken any specialist training that would equip me for that kind of role."

"You don't have to do anything you're uncomfortable with, and you can quit the placement anytime."

The doorbell rang.

"I've got to go Ben, someone's at the door."

She opened the door, as Ben said, "think about it and let me know."

"I don't have a choice," she said, "he's right here at my door."

Nick cocked his head and looked pleased with himself.

"Okay then, I'll get a panic button brooch delivered to you today."

"Fine," she said and hung up.

Nick stepped over the threshold, and closed the door behind him "that's right, I'm here."

"What do you want Nick?"

He raised the sketchbook to eye level, "I brought your book back."

She reached for it, but he pulled it out of her reach.

"Didn't I say you had to have a drink with me to get it back?" he arched an eyebrow at her.

And honestly, he looked gorgeous when he did that, but she just wanted to push him back out the door again.

Maybe that was why he'd shut it.

She sighed and rubbed her forehead. It was so much easier in her beige dress, sketching him from across the street.

Next job, she was requisitioning a camera like everyone else.

"Didn't I tell you I picked you out of a crowd because you're so beautiful?"

"I don't recall you saying any such thing."

He reached out to lightly touch her robe, "so nice to see what you're really like; in *living* colour."

In one smooth movement, she turned away so he missed touching her, but the robe slid down her shoulder, reminding her she was naked underneath it.

And still hadn't visited the little girl's room.

Which raised another issue. Her flat was a small studio apartment. More or less all that kept her living and sleeping rooms apart were a Chinese style screen and a bead curtain.

Luckily the bathroom had a door.

And enough space to hung a small load of handwashing to dry.

Unable to figure out how to get rid of him, she said "wait right *here*," and fled behind the screen.

Fortunately, in her line of work there was no room for "stage fright" - you might lose your target - so she got the bathroom thing out of the way lickedy-split.

She paused in front of the drying rack, thinking about what he'd said about living colour, and decided that if he wanted to get to know her, he would get to know the real her.

Not her quick disappear into a crowd work persona. It was about fine for eight hours of not being noticed, but as a woman of real, black and white opinions, hard to maintain.

Well, mostly the real her.

It would be dumb to let him get to know her.

She'd have to lie, and maybe when he found out about that, he'd back off. Fast.

She quickly dressed in mostly dry blue jeans and a red linen tunic.

When she got back to him, he wasn't *exactly* where she'd left him, but had taken two steps to the kitchen to make coffee for two.

Leaving her sketchbook on the table.

On the one hand annoying, but on the other, she *really* needed another coffee.

The doorbell rang, and he said, "I'll get that," almost sprinting to the door to his ubiquitous friend.

"Have you met Aresio?" Now that she looked at him, he would have seemed more attractive if he hadn't been standing next to Nick.

Funny that she hadn't really noticed him before; smooth blond hair, olive complexion, stunning blue eyes, with the same hidden, toned musculature. Something about him that seemed slightly menacing, now that she was giving him 100% of her focus.

But he wasn't the target, even if he was with him 95% of the time, and it was up to the analysts back in the office to identify and categorise him.

"Ares please," he said as he stepped into the flat, smiling at her then looking around, "nice place." He handed a bag of pastries that smelled divine to Nick and held out his hand.

"Ares," she took it, and his fingers tightened around hers, though whether he was trying to warn her, or size her up, or had noticed that she was somehow different from the day before she couldn't tell.

"All right, I'm out of here," he said, dropping her hand.

"You aren't staying?" she asked.

"And get in the way of you two love-birds? I don't think so.

"Besides, I've errands to run.

"Catch ya later!"

He turned and Nick transferred the bakery bag to his left hand and with his right, did a complicated handshake with Ares involving fist bumps, standard handshakes, thumb handshakes and shoulder taps.

And then she was alone with Nick.

At least she was fully dressed this time, but not sure whether to fold her hands in front of her groin, or fold her arms, or swing her arms or turn away.

"He's right," Nick said.

"About what?"

"It is a nice place, but not one where the beige version of you would be comfortable."

He went back into her little kitchen, put the pastries on a plate from the dish rack and started opening cupboards looking for another coffee cup, only there wasn't one.

"You have the cup, I'll take the glass," she went to the table to fetch it.

"You only have one cup?"

"I'm not here much."

"Why not?" he asked, pouring the coffee.

She gestured around the room, "I work a lot, and this place is too small to have many people around, so I just meet up elsewhere."

"Your cocoon," he looked around the flat again, this time noting the singles; one small couch, with one cushion and throw rug, one table.

One screen, partly obscuring a bed that hadn't been made yet.

And yet, it was comfortable, with art on the walls, and collections of shells, ceramics and tiny animal sculptures. And dammit he was right; it was her cocoon.

"Doesn't take much to clean," she said brightly.

He turned back to her.

She carried the plate to the table, and he carried the drinks.

They looked at each other and subsided into the couch.

Which only had one bum print in its centre, and as he settled on the left, and her on the right, the stuffing shifted throwing them closer together.

He cleared his throat and adjusted his seating a little further away.

"Are these yours?" he asked, gesturing at a couple of large landscapes she'd been trying to figure out how to use as room dividers.

She nodded.

"You're very talented." He looked around again, "may I look at your other sketchbooks?"

"No."

"Modest?"

"Not really, you can see there isn't much room here so I have a storage unit," she lied.

Wilkinson's bought the sketchbooks, new ones for each investigation so of course, she gave them back when they filled up.

He offered her the plate; she picked up a pastry and took a bite.

"You're the first person I've given a book to, but now I've got the idea I might be able to sell them," which was *technically* correct.

He chose a pastry and took a bite.

It occurred to her that she wasn't supposed to know anything about him, except that he was pretty enough to follow around for days trying to get a good picture.

And that she was getting a pay rise to find out more about him.

Which left her feeling uncomfortable, and a little dirty.

Even if he was a crime kingpin.

Clearly, she was not cut out for law enforcement.

"So, you know I go around drawing total strangers, what is it you do for a living?"

He laughed, "nothing as exciting as sketching strangers. I sell professional espresso coffee machines and supplies."

"Is it a good living?"

"Of course! This is Melbourne, home of the world's best coffee culture after all.

"Getting the distribution agreements with the overseas manufacturers was the hardest part, but pretty much everyone in business here is looking to buy or lease them.

"It's not just cafés and restaurants, I've got high-end boutiques, barbers and car repair services signed up too. I even had a plastic surgeon sign up for one yesterday!"

"A plastic surgeon? That's a road too far for me, but sometimes it can take hours at the hairdresser and I reckon a decent coffee would help the wait."

He ran a sticky finger along a lock of her hair, "you spend hours in a hairdresser to get this look?"

"It was for a wedding, okay?"

He stuffed the pasty in his mouth and held his hands out looking for something to wipe them with.

She swallowed the rest of her coffee, leaving the glass in the kitchen, brought him back the dish towel.

When she thought about it, every place she'd sketched him, sold coffee. It was a *very* good cover story.

The doorbell went, so she left him on the couch while she answered it.

"Package for delivery," Ryan said, "please sign here."

She stepped through to the corridor, and he quietly said, "it's a combined bug and panic button; I've activated it for you. If you can speak, say "Quetzalcoatl," and we'll know you're in trouble. Just press the head of the serpent to activate the alarm, and we'll come get you."

She nodded.

"Don't worry, we'll be nearby."

She smiled a thin, straight smile.

"Thanks very much," she called out as he left, and started unwrapping the parcel as she returned to the flat.

She shoved the wrapping in the pocket of her jeans, pinned the brooch to her right shoulder, and twisted her body back and forth, enjoying its sparkle in the changing light.

"That's pretty," Nick said, coming up behind her.

"I saw it online and paid full price before it could get away."

"Is that Quetzalcoatl?"

She didn't start, or pause, just said, "sure is," as she took his hand and walked back to the couch, settling in on his left where, hopefully, the bug would pick him up well.

"Tell me more about your coffee business."

Nick smiled, as though it was a topic he couldn't get enough of.

"Well, if I was selling you one, I'd want to know how many cups you'd be making, what kinds of coffee, and how much effort to put into them."

"And want if I didn't want to make any effort at all?"

"Then I'd get you the fully automatic push-button kind and have it plumbed into the main water pipe. Then you'd just have to fill up the milk powder and sugar when it ran out."

"What if I wanted to make "proper" lattes for people?"

"If you were making coffees all day, then I'd suggest a machine with a heat exchanger, or if you were really concerned about an exact temperature of coffee a multi-boiler.

"You need something like 25 amps of power for the heat exchanger and up to 40 for a boiler.

"And a two-group head for about 20 kg of coffee a week, or three groups for up to 100 kg a week.

"You've got machines where you can program shots by weight, and others that auto-brew.

"Plus, I'd recommend an automatic cleaning cycle and an overnight mode that powers down when you haven't used it for a while.

"And let's not forget the ergonomic stress of using it all, so you want to think about bench height, and comfortable handles, and antifatigue mats."

"Or coffee for twelve in one go?"

"Drip filter style. The beauty of this kind is that you don't need to plug it in the main water, just add fresh water."

It sounded plausible, but he hadn't said anything she couldn't have figured out by herself with an internet search.

And she didn't have enough knowledge to ask him the right questions to trap him.

"What about Ares?"

"I saved his life, and when he fell on hard times, I hired him; he drives me around, helps me move the stock, and does other bits and pieces."

She nodded, plausible.

"What about you? What kind of job do you have that gives you the time to follow me around for days?"

"Actually, I've fallen on hard times myself - I'm between jobs. Taking a week off before looking for something else."

She hated lying, but how else was she supposed to explain it? It wasn't the kind of thing "normal" people did.

They sat silently for a moment. Nick looked around again, and Susan was relieved she hadn't room for anything much more than small, secondhand furniture. There wasn't anything there to suggest a good job, just junk.

If he asked what kind of job, what should she say?

Or would he be worried she was going to ask him for a job?

He cleared his throat again. "So, who was on the phone then?"

"When?"

"Just then, you said 'I don't have a choice, he's right here at my door.'"

And reminded her of the stakes again.

Nick Liang was supposed to be the kind of guy who would beat you up as soon as look at you.

She had to remember that, no matter how nice and, well, innocent he seemed.

"Oh that," she manufactured a giggle, "I was just telling my friend about you. She was warning me to steer clear."

They smiled at each other for a moment.

Susan, forgetting for a moment she was drinking from a glass she'd left in the kitchen, lunged for his coffee before he could do something worrying, like kiss her.

His phone rang, breaking the tension and bring some breathing space.

He glanced at it, and said, "sorry, I have to get this," before getting off the couch and walking out the door.

She snuck after him, trying to eavesdrop on the conversation.

"Yes," he said, followed by grunting interspersed by periods when someone at the other end said something.

Difficult to read much into that, until he said, "I'll be there as soon as I can."

Fortunately, she had enough time to get into the kitchen and look like she was busy.

"I'm sorry," he said, "I've got to go. There's a thing..."

"Oh. Well. Okay then. I'll see you sometime."

"Can, um, can I call you?"

"What, oh yeah, I guess."

And then, blessedly, he was gone.

Presumably taking Ryan and whoever had replaced her on surveillance detail.

Leaving a space behind that was ridiculously big for someone who'd barely been there an hour.

But having been that close to him, she didn't think he the same air of lethality Aresio did.

The original team briefing hadn't detailed much of the kind of information you'd think a person who'd killed another person with his bare hands would accrue.

It was as if he'd suddenly appeared, with no gang affiliation or history to explain who he was and where he'd come from.

He'd emerged fully formed out of nowhere. Without a supervillain origin story if you will.

She decided to do some digging on her own, and pulled her laptop out from its storage place under the couch, logging into her account at Wilkinson's and searching all the databases available to her; publicly and through Wilkinson's subscriptions.

Sometime later, she'd come with back plenty over the last five years or so, and next to nothing previously.

Not high school records, not immigration records, not even a library card.

It would have done for the most cursory background check, but not for someone like her, or someone using the specialised skills at Wilkinson's.

For comparison, she searched Aresio, found a number of aliases, criminal activity dating back more than a decade, as well as school records.

She rang Mimma, who asked, "how are you getting on with the target? Any issues I need to know about?"

"Fine, he's left me to do something, but I expect Ryan is tailing him.

"But something's not right, and I'm not sure I can explain it."

"What makes you say that?"

Susan settled herself more comfortably on the couch, "what exactly do we know about our client, and what exactly do we know about Nick Liang?"

"We haven't backgrounded the client, and our basic starting point is always that the client is honest with us. The fee for engagement generally ensures only serious queries."

"Has anyone authorised a full background search on Nick Liang to confirm the details we've been given?"

"I couldn't say for sure, that wasn't part of my briefing. Why?"

"I've done some basic background, and his history is quite short. On the other hand, his friend Aresio Vitale has a long history."

"What are you saying?" Mimma was starting to sound annoyed.

"I'm wondering whether Nick Liang exists, or whether he's an undercover operative sent by the AFP, or ASIO.

"Perhaps to investigate Aresio?"

Mimma was silent, Susan could almost hear Mimma's brain moving.

Susan continued, "the client may be suspicious of Nick's credentials, and if he's undercover, we may be putting his life in danger."

Susan waited another moment or two before Mimma sighed.

"Let me check with Ben. I'll get back to you."

It was several days before she heard from Mimma, but in the meantime, she'd watched the news break as the AFP busted an international drug ring in conjunction with Police in 16 other countries.

They'd seized more than 105 kg of drugs, 42 firearms, more than 9.5 million dollars in cash, plus luxury goods and cars in Victoria alone. As well as evidence of 19 murder plots in ongoing investigations.

Prominent footage included Aresio wearing handcuffs, escorted by Police, plus others with covers over their heads.

No sign or mention of Nick though.

And when she got her next pay, it included exactly 2.8 days of higher duties, most of which was gobbled up in the extra tax.

According to Mimma, Ben had contacted someone he knew in the intelligence community, and shared some information about the investigation. And that was about all she permitted to know.

Presumably, they'd gotten him out.

«« • »»

Life continued pretty much as normal. She took her sketchbooks from Wilkinson's and dressed in her beige sundress as she continued to sketch her assigned targets.

As the weather cooled, she added a beige cardigan and sought warmer observation points than benches in the Bourke Street Mall.

She tried harder to blend into the crowds, but her heart wasn't really in it.

And she kept seeing Nick everywhere. Though she was fairly sure that was her imagination.

He'd given her a glimpse of an alternative future. Not so much the gangster's moll element, more the like-minded... Soul mate?

Gak.

She definitely needed a holiday somewhere sunny and frenzied, followed by a transfer to another department.

Someone took a seat next to her, but as the café was filling up for the lunch crowd, she just shifted her chair enough to clear her view of the target.

"Did you forget me so soon?" a voice asked?

She looked up to see Nick. Only also not Nick.

He'd cut his hair, and dressed in jeans and a button-down shirt with the sleeves rolled up, looked less like a gangster and more like the Police officer she'd supposed him to be.

"You still owe me a drink," he said.

She didn't know what to say, so she didn't say anything.

He stood up and offered her his hand.

She looked past him to Ryan on the other side of the café, and made a seemingly random coded gesture to let him know she was off.

Then looked back up at Nick, and said "fine.

"You owe me an explanation."

"If I didn't owe you my life, I'd be demanding an explanation."

She smiled, and took his hand, "let's get a drink and you can tell me all about it."

THE END

ABOUT THE AUTHOR

Alexandria Blaelock writes stories, some of them for *Ellery Queen's Mystery Magazine* and *Pulphouse Fiction Magazine.*

She's also written five self-help books applying business techniques to personal matters like getting dressed, cleaning house, and feeding your friends.

She lives in a forest because she enjoys birdsong, and the smell of gum leaves. When not telecommuting to parallel universes from her Melbourne based imagination, she watches K-dramas, talks to animals, and drinks Campari. At the same time.
Discover more at www.alexandriablaelock.com.

... or the first Georgia Garside

The Robin Hood of Private Investigators

Georgia Garside. Foul-mouthed Private Investigator. Ex-contorionist.

Out of her depth. In over her head.

Caught up in the war between a wealthy industrialist and the ex-sugar babe who can't take a hint.

A laugh-out-loud tripartite battle of wits, winner takes all.

www.ingramcontent.com/pod-product-compliance
Lightning Source LLC
Chambersburg PA
CBHW030813190726
48285CB00003B/1159